"**Rumiko Takahashi** doesn't miss a single farcical opportunity as every volume is crammed with raging hormones, romantic entanglements, gender-swapping, and martial-art silliness. Boy changes to girl, man to panda, girl to cat -- and everybody's kung fu fighting."

Anodyne Magazine

"If you've never watched any of the videos, or read the comic books they are based on, you're missing out on some of the funniest, wackiest, and most character-driven cartoons around."

Tony Isabella, comics critic

"**Ranma 1/2** is a must for anyone who likes a wicked sense of humor."

Gamers' Republic

OTHER TITLES BY RUMIKO TAKAHASHI

RANMA 1/2
MAISON IKKOKU
LUM*URUSEI YATSURA
INU-YASHA
RUMIC WORLD TRILOGY
RUMIC THEATER
ONE-POUND GOSPEL
MERMAID SAGA

VIZ GRAPHIC NOVEL

RANMA 1/2

STORY & ART BY

RUMIKO TAKAHASHI

CONTENTS

This volume contains the second half of RANMA 1/2 PART THREE, #7 through RANMA 1/2 PART THREE, #13 in their entirety.

Story & Art by Rumiko Takahashi

*

Translation/Gerard Jones & Toshifumi Yoshida & Matt Thorn
Touch-Up Art & Lettering/Wayne Truman
Cover Design/Viz Graphics
Editor/Trish Ledoux
Assistant Editors/Annette Roman & Toshifumi Yoshida

*

Managing Editor/Satoru Fujii
Director of Sales & Marketing/Oliver Chin
Executive Editor/Seiji Horibuchi
Publisher/Keizo Inoue

*

First Published by Shogakukan, Inc. in Japan

*

Printed in Canada

*

Published by Viz Communications, Inc.
P.O. Box 77010
San Francisco, CA 94107

*

10 9 8 7 6
First printing, September 1995
Sixth printing, August 1999

Part One

KITTEN OF THE SEA

AAR RGH!
FWISH FWISH
GLRBL URBL
MWAAAA
NO, NO, NO! WITH AKANE WEIGHING HIM DOWN...
GAME IS OVER!

EEEE!
UNGH!
SHARK-FIST!

RANMA, IS REALLY TIME YOU GIVE UP.
YOU CAN'T BEAT GREAT-GRANDMOTHER.
SHHH
SHE'S RIGHT!
ACKNOWLEDGE DEFEAT AND BECOME SHAMPOO'S GROOM!
PLOOSH
I CAN WIN.

IF *YOU'RE* WITH ME, SHAMPOO...I CAN BEAT ANYONE!
YOU'LL HELP ME, WON'T YOU?
HUH? HUH?
WON'T YOU?
WON'T YOU?
WON'T YOU?

YOU REALLY NEED ME, RANMA?
SIGH
IT CAN ONLY BE YOU!
RANMA!

AND I SUPPOSE *I'D* ONLY GET IN THE WAY!
WELL, I'M GLAD TO SEE YOU AGREE!
PROMISE ME, SHAMPOO...NO MATTER WHAT, YOU WON'T LET GO OF ME!
OOO, I PROMISE!
CINCH
YOU DIDN'T HAVE TO HIT HIM THAT HARD!

I'M COMING, GHOUL!
...JUST BECAUSE YOU DRAGGED SHAMPOO INTO THIS!
HMPH. DON'T THINK I'LL GO EASY ON YOU...
SHOOM
SHOOM

PLORSH

OKAY, FINE, SO I'M A LEAD WEIGHT IN THE WATER!
BUT WHAT ABOUT SHAMPOO? WHEN SHE'S IN THE WATER, SHE TURNS INTO...
OH!

MLLEOW?
BLUB BLUB

RANMA!
HE'S RESORTING TO THE CAT-FIST!
"CAT-FIST"?

THE UNBEATABLE TECHNIQUE OF BECOMING A CAT--AND FIGHTING WITH A CAT'S FEROCITY!
HE CAN WIN THIS YET!

FSHHHH
COME NOW, GROOM, WHAT'S THE MATTER?
PLASH PLASH
MYEW MYEW
WAAAAA!

WAAAAA!
PLASH PLASH
MYEW MYEW
FSHHHH

"UNBEATABLE TECHNIQUE," HUH?
...

WAAAAA!
BLASH
BLASH
BLASH
BLASH
MYEW MYEW
WOULD YOU PLEASE...

WHAT'S WRONG WITH HER?

MRRROWR!

FFFT!

AH!

THAT POSE! CAN IT BE...?

YOWWWLLL
SPROING
SHARK-FIST!
POOM
ROWR! ROWR! ROWR!
WHAP WHAP WHAP
SPSHHH

SHHHAP
YOWR YOWR
OHHH
AMAZING!
THE WATER'S PEELING OFF LIKE WOOD SHAVINGS!
BLASH BLASH
FSHHH
SSHHHHHHH

FWOP

RRRRRR
OH HH!

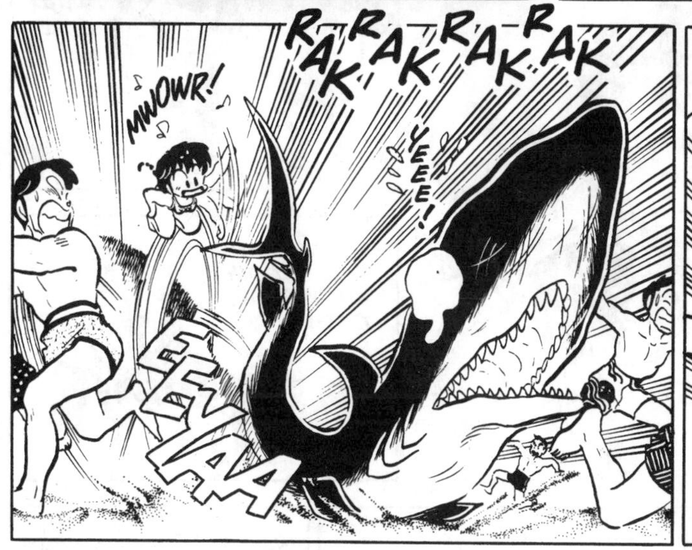
RAK RAK RAK RAK
MWOWR!
YEEEE!
EEYAA

RANMA!
THAT'S ENOUGH!

RRRT?
LOOK OUT! SHE'S DANGEROUS!

MYOWW!
BOING
OH!

PAP

NICE KITTY, NICE KITTY.
PRRR
PRRR
PRRR

BRRR! WHAT TERROR!
SHE'S... SHE'S CALM!

SO. TO THINK THE GROOM KNOWS THE CAT-FIST!

DO YOU STILL INTEND TO FIGHT?
WAIT!
FFFF!

NO ONE'S GIVEN ME SUCH TROUBLE IN FIFTY YEARS!
HSSST!

SPOP
PHOENIX PILL
THERE.

HA HA HA HA HA HA!
WE'LL MEET AGAIN!
A PRIZE... FOR A FIGHTING SPIRIT!
THE PHOENIX PILL!
PHOENIX PILL

SHHHHHH H

...KISSED YOU...
I COULD'VE JUST KICKED...
WHEN YOU JUMPED IN AND NEARLY KILLED...
...SAVED ME...
SO... THANKS. REALLY.
AKANE, YOU DUH... DUH...
DEAR.
INN

NO POINT GETTING FANCY.
URG.
HSSSSS

I'VE JUST GOTTA SAY IT!
OKAY.

THANKS FOR WHAT YOU DID.

AK!
YOU WELCOME!
BUT OF COURSE I HELP MY GROOM!
BLOOSH

I'VE ONLY JUST BEGUN, GROOM!
HEH HEH HEH HEH HEH
SHAMPOO, I THINK IT'S TIME WE HAD A TALK ABOUT BATHTUBS AND MEN.
POOR RANMA SEE ME AND PASS OUT!
WHY SHOULD HE?! AFTER ALL, WHAT GOOD AM I?!
RANMA! AREN'T YOU GOING TO THANK AKANE?!
RRIP!

Part Two

CARE TO JOIN ME?

MAIL'S HERE!
CHREEEE CHREEEE
A CHALLENGE ?!
AHA! FROM RYOGA!
I AM TRAINING IN THE MOUNTAINS.
TOMORROW I SHALL COME TO TENDO HALL.
PREPARE TO MEET YOUR DOOM!

A WEEK LATER...

CHREEEE
CHREEEE

EEE-YAAA! HOT HOT HOT HOT!

BLOOSH

AI-YAAA...

BLUH

OH?

HYAH.

FUWOOOP

KLONG

SO. YOU ARE A FRIEND OF THE GROOM.

I AM NOT HIS FRIEND!

IT IS RANMA SAOTOME'S FAULT THAT I TURN INTO A *PIG!*

SHH SHH SHH

OH, SO?

WHAT DO YOU SAY?

WILL YOU JOIN ME?

JUST WHAT DO YOU MEAN?

I AM OFFERING TO TRAIN YOU.

FEH.

DON'T BE ABSURD.

YOU'RE WALKING OUT ON ME?

I'M NOT SO WEAK THAT I NEED TRAINING FROM SOME OLD LADY.

TA-TA, GRANNY.

I'D LIKE TO GIVE ONE TO MR. TENDO.

CAN YOU TAKE IT WITH YOU?

HUH?

SHWA
PREPARE TO *DIE,* *RANMA!*
HEY, RYOGA.
YOU'RE A WEEK LATE.

NOW FIGHT!
JAB JAB JAB
WHOA!
HOLD IT!

I HAVE TO DELIVER THIS!
IS THAT SO?
WELL, THEN...
JAB
JAB

IF I ELIMINATE WHAT YOU NEED TO DELIVER...
THEN YOU CAN FIGHT WITH A CLEAR CONSCIENCE, CAN'T YOU?
VISH
WATCH IT!

STOP THAT SQUIRMING!
VISH
.....
VISH

AA!
TSK TSK.
YOU'RE GETTING SLOW, RYOGA!
VMM

YOU REALLY *ARE* SLOW!
BOFF
THMP

HOW *DARE* YOU MOCK ME?!
JAB
MAN !

TH-THIS CANNOT BE!

BA-BUMP
A... A... AKANE!
OH, HI, RYOGA.
WAK !!
ARROT
ZIP
PINCH
SCREECH

ARE YOU TWO FIGHTING AGAIN?
I MEAN, REALLY...
WHAT AM I SUPPOSED TO DO?
RYOGA KEEPS ATTACKING ME!
HUMILIATING ME IN FRONT OF AKANE LIKE THIS! THIS IS UNPARDONABLE! THIS MUST NOT BE!
GRRRRR
DOW YOU WILL BAY!
VOOM
UNGRATEFUL JERK!
BAPPITA BAPPIT

BY THE WAY, AKANE...
HAVE YOU FOUND YOUR LITTLE PET PIGGY YET?
P-CHAN...?
WELL, I HAVE BEEN LOOKING FOR HIM, BUT...
WHAT MAKES YOU ASK?
YOU WANNA SEE HIM?
VOOP
GYAAAA!

STOP PICKING ON POOR RYOGA!
BOOT
THWIP
OUCH!
WHO'S PICKING ON WHO?!
FLIP
PLAP

WAIT A SECOND!

RANMA'S SUCH A JERK!
HE SHOULD HAVE TAKEN IT EASY ON YOU!
LET ME SEE. THIS JOINT GOES LIKE THIS...
KRR-RAK
SNAP
OR DOES IT GO... OH, I DON'T KNOW!
ANYWAY, RYOGA, I THINK IT'D BE BETTER IF YOU DIDN'T CHALLENGE RANMA ANYMORE.

HE DOESN'T KNOW IT, BUT FROM ALL THOSE FIGHTS WITH SHAMPOO'S GREAT-GRANDMOTHER...
...HE'S GOTTEN MUCH STRONGER AND FASTER.
SO YOU'D BE BETTER OFF...

NO! I DON'T WANT TO SEE PITY IN THOSE EYES!

WHAT--?!
RYOGA !!
Fwap Fwap
I WON'T HAVE IT!

DAMN YOU!
DAMN YOU!
TAK
TAK
TAK
DAMN YOU!

DAMN YOU, RANMA!
WAK

6420
SO. IT LOOKS AS THOUGH YOU'VE BEEN MADE TO PLAY THE FOOL.

I WAS THINKING HOW I'D LIKE TO TALK TO YOU AGAIN.
.....
HYOOOOO
FUNNY...
...I WAS JUST THINKING THE SAME THING.

Part Three

TRAINING MEALS

HONESTLY!

TWITTER

TWITTER

CHREE

CHREE

CHREE

WHHHHOK

IT'S SUMMER VACATION, FOR PITY'S SAKE!

WHOK

HOW COULD I GET STUCK WITH THIS?

YOU MUST ACCOMPANY RANMA ON HIS TRAINING JOURNEY AND TAKE CARE OF THE COOKING.

IT'LL BE GOOD TRAINING FOR WHEN YOU GET MARRIED, AKANE.

"TRAINING" FOR ***MARRIAGE!*** HMPH!

WHHOK

Za

WHY DIDN'T YOU SAY *NO*, POP ?!

Za

CHOP CHOP CHOP

HOW'M I SUPPOSED TO TRAIN WITH A GIRL TAGGING ALONG?

Your cooking is horrible!

Za

Za

RIGHT, LIKE YOU'RE A REAL GOURMET.

GROOM! WHAT A SURPRISE!

ARE YOU IN TRAINING TOO?

BOING

BRRRRR!

!

TICKLE

NO! NOT YOU AGAIN!
JAB
WHOOSH.
DON'T MISUNDERSTAND.
I DIDN'T COME TO FIGHT YOU.

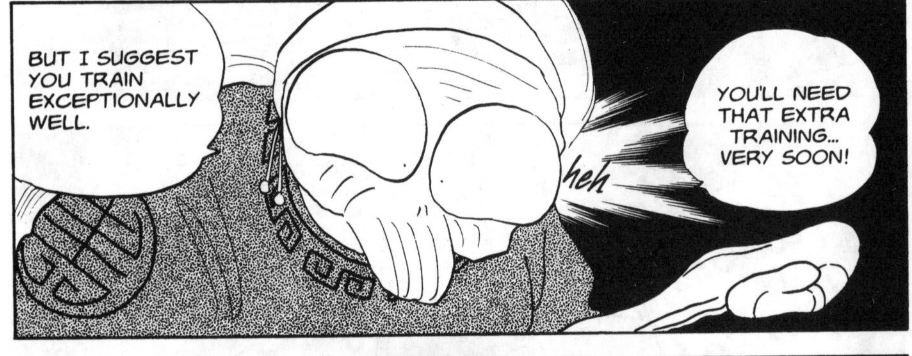

BEFORE WE BEGIN...
HHHSHHHHH
IS THAT ALL?
I WANT TO SEE YOU SHATTER THIS BOULDER.
MIGHTY CONFIDENT, AREN'T WE?
HEH-HEH.
AND HERE I WAS WONDERING WHAT ARDUOUS TRAINING YOU WOULD PUT ME THROUGH!
KRAK KRAK

YES!!
SHOK
HOW'S THAT?
KRAK
FINE. EXCEPT I DIDN'T SAY "SPLIT IT."
I SAID I WANTED TO SEE YOU *SHATTER* IT.
LIKE THIS.
SHHHHHH
TP

.....
KRRMBBLL

CARE TO LEARN THAT TRICK?

BONG
AND I THOUGHT NOTHING ABOUT YOU COULD SHOCK ME MORE THAN YOUR *FACE*.

MAN, I'M STARVED.

SO! CURRY TONIGHT, EH?

IT MAY NOT LOOK LIKE MUCH, BUT...

BUBBLE BUBBLE

WELL. HERE.

PLOP

IT SMELLS... INTER-ESTING.

CAN YOU TELL? I ADDED SOME WHITE WINE!

COME ON, THEN, LET'S DIG IN!

CHOMP

CHOMP

.....
THANKS FOR DINNER!
ZZZZZMMMM

YES SIR!
VOOM
WELL, SON, TIME WE GOT BACK TO TRAINING!

poit

URKH.
GLURRGLL

HMM. MAYBE IT'S THE WINE THAT DIDN'T WORK. WHAT KIND OF...

VINEGAR.
Vinegar

GRRR GRRR
DIDN'T I TELL YOU NOT TO BRING HER?!
YOU'RE HER FIANCÉ! WHY DON'T YOU MAKE SURE SHE KNOWS HOW TO COOK?!

RANMA, YOU ARE SUCH A...
GRNT

THAT'S STILL NO REASON TO RUN OUT ON ME!
DIDN'T I DO MY BEST FOR HIM?

JERK!
VISH
KRAK

KRUNCH
FUMP
PWOR
OH!
RYOGA!

HISHHHH

TAKE CARE OF THE CAMP FOR ME.
I'M GOING DOWN THE MOUNTAIN FOR NEW PROVISIONS.
LOUSY FATHER, RUNNING OFF AND LEAVING ME LIKE THAT.

WHO COULD STICK AROUND TO EAT THAT SO-CALLED "FOOD" OF HERS.
BUT MAN...
GROWWLLLL

BOING
BOING
CURSE YOU, AKANE!
ONLY A STARVING IDIOT LIKE *ME!*

HUH? RYOGA!
SO YOU'RE HERE TO TRAIN, TOO?
BUBBLE
BUBBLE
BUBBLE
WELL, AS YOU SAW, I WAS NOT QUITE GOOD ENOUGH BEFORE.

HMM, WONDER IF THAT HELPED ANY...?
plop

UM...HERE. BUT I DON'T KNOW IF IT'S...
OF COURSE IT'S GOOD!

SOBB
SNIF
SNIF
SNIF
OH, IT'S GOOD TO BE ALIVE!
TO EAT THE HOME COOKING OF THE BEAUTEOUS AKANE!
THERE CAN BE NO HAPPIER MAN!

THANK YOU, AKANE!
BLORCH!

FWAP
FWAP
FWAP
hoo
hoo
hoo

UHH
UHH
UHH

I GUESS...
IT ISN'T SO GOOD ?

N-N-NEVER IN MY L-LIFE HAVE I TASTED...
TWITCH TWITCH
ANYTHING S-S-S-SO EXQUISITE!

OH, GOODIE !
I *KNEW* THE MAYONNAISE AND SUGAR WOULD HELP!
WHUMP
TWITCH TWITCH TWITCH
BONK.

RANMA!
WHO SAID YOU COULD HAVE ANY?!
VIP
DUH... DO YOU TUH-TASTE IT...
BEFORE YOU SUH-SERVE IT?

NO. WHY?
I SUGGEST YOU DO! PLEASE!

ARE YOU SAYING IT'S BAD?!
TASTE IT AND YOU'LL SEE!

PONG

I WILL NOT SIT QUIETLY AND LISTEN TO THIS.
HUH?
YOU PICKING A FIGHT?

PLEASE RYOGA, DON'T!
YOU SAID IT WAS GOOD, AND THAT'S WHAT COUNTS!
HE DIDN'T HURT ME AT ALL!

I REALLY DON'T LIKE PICKING ON WEAKER GUYS, YOU KNOW.
JERK
WEAKER...?
WHY, YOU--
VOOM

PINK

PONK

GHOUL, WHAT...?
THE FIGHT WILL BE IN ONE WEEK.
FOMP
TOK

JUST YOU WAIT, GROOM.
YOU WILL HAVE A FORMIDABLE OPPONENT!
HEH HEH
......

I HAVE TO LOOK AFTER RYOGA!
HUH?
AKANE, WAIT!

RYOGA HAPPENS TO *LIKE* MY COOKING!

CURSE YOU, AKANE!
I CAN LEARN TO LIKE THIS SLOP, TOO! I CAN!
RANMA, ENOUGH ALREADY.
YOU LOOK LIKE YOU'RE ABOUT TO DIE.

Part Four

THE BREAKING POINT

CHRP
CHRRP
HAAAHH!
KRAKKL
SWISHHH

SHOOOO

HYAAAAA!

THOK

TIP
YOU HAVE TO HIT THE *BREAKING POINT!*
TOP
HOW MANY TIMES MUST I TELL YOU?!
KRACH
TAK
YOW!
TAK
TAK
THAT BOULDER...

WHAT A TECHNIQUE.
IF RYOGA EVER MASTERS THAT...
SPASH KA CASH
TOKKA TOKKA
...RANMA WILL BE...
SPLAT
THUD

SO, SON-IN-LAW.
COME TO CHECK UP ON US?
NOT PARTIC-ULARLY.
SHHF
FUD
FAP
OH, RYOGA!
VOOM
ARE YOU ALL RIGHT?
OH, POOR RYOGA.
.....

WAH HA HA HA HA HA HA HA HA!
WAH HA HA HA HA HA HA! TOSSED ASIDE BY YOUR GIRL, EH, BOY?

I'LL SEE YOU.
WHERE ARE YOU GOING?
I THOUGHT YOU CAME HERE TO TAKE BACK YOUR LITTLE FIANCÉE!
.....

Y-YOU WERE?
I WAS JUST WORRIED, THAT'S ALL!

AKANE...

YES...?

YOU... YOU... YOU...
HE AND I HAVE A FIGHT COMING UP.
DON'T POISON HIM WITH YOUR COOKING.
PAT PAT

BOOOM
...R-R-RANMA!!
OFF HE RUNS.
SUCH A FICKLE YOUNG MAN.
DON'T YOU THINK YOU SHOULD SWITCH TO RYOGA?
.....

RANMA... WHAT WILL HAPPEN TO YOU?
HE REALLY MEANS IT!
BREAKING A BOULDER WITH ONE FINGER?!
WHAT?!
CAWW CAWW
CAWW
BREAKING POINT?
IT MUST BE THE SECRET BREAKING POINT TECHNIQUE!

...OR, YES... THE HUMAN BODY!

SO IF HE DOESN'T TOUCH ME, HE CAN'T HURT ME.

NO SWEAT.

WELL...

BZZ

BZZ.

BZZ...

...WE'LL SEE ABOUT THAT!
WHOK
BUZZ
GAK!

ZZZZZZZZZZ
KNOCK DOWN ALL THE BEES WITHOUT BEING STUNG...

HEH.
NOTHING TO IT!
VISHH
POP POP POP
POP POP POP

HWOOO

DON'T STRAIN YOURSELF.
SHUT UP!
BZZ.. BZZ.. BZZ..

YOU'LL SEE, YOU STUPID AKANE!
THERE'S NO WAY I'M GOING TO LOSE!

WHISSHHH!

POKE
POKE
HEEEEE-YAAA!
POKE POKE
POKE POKE

AKH!

VOOM

NOT GOOD ENOUGH!

YOU CANNOT FIND THE BREAKING POINT WITH OTHER THINGS ON YOUR MIND!

I DON'T HAVE ANYTHING ELSE ON MY MIND!

.....

SHWING

.....

AKANE

ZZZZZ

HEY!

WHAT'S THE *BIG IDEA?!*

I JUST THOUGHT THE FIGHT WOULD BE BETTER IF THERE WERE A PRIZE AT STAKE.

PRIZE ?!

DOOM

PREPARE TO DIE!

Part Five

THE IMMORTAL MAN

HWOOOOOO
FASHION EYE
UNDER WEAR
SHA!
NOW, RANMA !!

JAB
JUKE
FOR SOMEBODY TRAINED BY THAT GHOUL...
KLOP
...YOU LEAVE A LOT OF OPENINGS!

TOPP
THEN I'LL SEE TO IT...
...THAT YOUR OPEN MOUTH IS CLOSED FOREVER!
THE *BREAKING POINT!*
KOOM

TALK IS CHEAP!
TK
TK
VISH
TK
IS THIS A SMOKE SCREEN?
VISH
HYAH!
YEP!
FOOM
TOO BAD YOU MISSED!

WITH THIS TECH- NIQUE...
RANMA ACTUALLY HAS THE ADVANTAGE!
RYOGA'S ALWAYS AT THE POINT OF THE "BLAST"...
...SO *HE* GETS HAMMERED BY THE ROCK SHRAPNEL!
WHILE HIS TARGET, RANMA...
...GETS OFF MUCH EASIER!
BUT WHY WOULD THE OLD WOMAN TEACH SUCH A THING?
I THOUGHT SHE WANTED *RYOGA* TO WIN!

SNORT
SOON ENOUGH, THE GROOM WILL LEARN...
...THE TERRIFYING TRUE POWER OF THE BREAKING POINT TECHNIQUE!
JAB
IF YOU TAKE MANY MORE ROCKS, YOU'RE NOT GONNA MAKE IT.
JAB
STUFF IT!
VIP
MAYBE I SHOULD END THIS...
KWAP
... RIGHT NOW!
THAT'S... IT?!

SLAM
KRAK
KRAK
KRONCH
TOK
TOK
TOK
TOK
HUH.
EASIER THAN I THOUGHT.

KRAKL
AKL
AKL
HUH?!
WAK !!
KROOM
GLOMP
TOK
TOK
TOK
KUH
RAK

HA HA HA HA HA HA HA HA!
YOU'VE GOTTEN WEAK, RANMA!
SHOOOOM

WHAT ?!

YOUR KICK FELT LIKE THE TOUCH OF A *BABY'S* FOOT!

IT CAN'T BE!

WAIT! NOW I SEE!
RYOGA'S TRAINING MADE HIM TOUGHER AGAINST IMPACTS!

CAN YOU DEFEAT RYOGA NOW...?
NOW WHAT, SON-IN-LAW?
BOINK
OLD GHOUL...

I'VE TRAINED TOO!
I CAN TAKE HIM ANYTIME!

BUT...
PROBABLY ALL YOU DID WAS PRACTICE DODGING.
GLURK

YOU FORGET?

I HAPPEN TO BE THE PRIZE IN THIS FIGHT.

IT'S NOT LIKE I'M FIGHTING TO WIN *YOU!*

BLAHHH

GRRRR

RYOGA'S WAITING FOR YOU DOWN BELOW.

SNIP

BOOT
...TOUCH ME!
WHAT'D YOU DO THAT FOR?!
DON'T... YOU...
WHSSHHH
!
SHOOOM
POIK
HEH

KLOP
BREAKING POINT BLOCK!
HEY!
VIP
KLOP
TRRK
WITH BOTH HANDS BLOCKED...
TRRK TRRK

WHOK WHOK WHOK
YOU'RE MINE !!
AS I SAID, YOUR KICKS ARE JUST...
TONK
...LIKE A BABY'S !!
SHUDO
YOU DON'T HAVE THE STRENGTH...

FAK
FAK
...TO STOP ME, RANMA!
UGH!
TAK
TAK
I DIDN'T WANT TO HAVE TO USE THIS, RYOGA!
THE SAOTOME SECRET TECHNIQUE!
THE WHAT ?!
WILL HE REALLY USE IT ?!
?!

Part Six
FAST BREAK

THE SAOTOME SECRET TECHNIQUE ?!

WHISH

TWIST

FACE OPPONENT AND...

SCREECH
...FAST BREAK !!

THAT...
VOOOOOMM

..."SECRET TECHNIQUE"?!
HWOOOOO

...WAS THE SAOTOME...

VOOOOOM
COME BACK HERE, YOU COWARD !!

TWONG TWONG
LISTEN WELL, MY SON...
THE SECRET TECHNIQUE OF THE SAOTOME CLAN...
...IS FOUNDED UPON THE TENETS OF "MOTION", "CONTEMPLATION" AND "OPPOSITION."

IN OTHER WORDS, RUNNING AWAY TO BUY YOURSELF TIME TO THINK ABOUT HOW TO ATTACK YOUR ENEMY.
BINGO!

WHAT KIND OF "TECHNIQUE" IS THAT?!
Hey, it's harder than it looks!

FEH. THE FOOL!
AS IF RUNNING INTO THE WOODS WILL MAKE ANY DIFFERENCE!
SNAP SNAP

TWANG

JUST 'CAUSE YOU'VE GOTTEN A LITTLE TOUGHER, RYOGA...

BADDAP
KRAK
WHOK
THAT TICKLES!
NGH?!

SO IT TICKLES, EH?!
......
WOBBLE
ODD.
THE RECOIL OF A BRANCH SHOULDN'T DO THAT!
VOOM
YOU WILL REGRET THIS--
BRRRT
WITH NO BRANCH THIS TIME!

WAIT! IT LOOKS LIKE A SINGLE PUNCH!

BUT HE'S ACTUALLY HITTING THE SAME SPOT HUNDREDS OF TIMES!

NO WONDER RYOGA'S FEELING IT!

WHAK!

SHHHHHHH

THE LONGER THIS FIGHT LASTS... THE MORE CERTAIN THE GROOM IS TO LOSE.

WHAT ?!

Top

BUT RANMA'S ALREADY WON!

YOOOOM

!

AT LEAST YOU MADE THIS FIGHT WORTHWHILE.
HEH...
THIS GUY'S A MONSTER!
YAA!
huf huf huf
BRRRT
UH-OH.
PREPARE YOURSELF, RANMA!
VOOOOOM
huf huf
huf huf
BREATHING A LITTLE HARD, AREN'T YOU?
SCFF

WHAT'S WRONG, RANMA?! YOU CAN'T BE TIRED AFTER JUST THROWING A FEW HUNDRED PUNCHES!
JAB
AK!
JAB
YOW!
HE'S RIGHT...
I'VE ONLY GOT ONE GOOD ROUND OF THOSE LEFT IN ME!
I GOTTA MAKE THIS ONE COUNT!
ZHAB
WHUMP
YOU DUMMY!
HOW COULD YOU FALL DOWN NOW?!
BREAKING POINT!

BWOOOM
TOK
VISH
CLOMP
TAK
CLOMP
TAK TAK

SO HOW 'BOUT...
BRRRRR!
...THIS ONE?!
RAT
UGH
I GOT...
KRAK...
...YOU?!

SCREEECH
RANMA!
FWAP FWAP
EEEEEEYOW!!!

huf
huf
PLISH
PLOOSH
SHHUMP
BLAST IT, RYOGA...
WHY D'YOU HAFTA BE SO MUCH TROUBLE?
PLOP

RELAX, GROOM!
"BREAKING POINT" WAS DEVELOPED FOR THE CON-STRUCTION INDUSTRY. IT ONLY WORKS ON ROCKS.
HEY! ARE YOU LISTENING TO ME?
I SAID, "ONLY ROCKS." IT CAN'T HURT PEOPLE.
BRRR BRRR
GRR GRR GRR

AND SO...

SAY GOODBYE TO AKANE FOR ME.
I ACCEPT MY DEFEAT GRACEFULLY THIS TIME, RANMA.

RANMA! P-CHAN'S FINALLY COME HOME!
I WON'T HAVE YOU MAKING HIM FEEL UNWELCOME!
HEY, PIG, WHAT IS THIS?
WEREN'T YOU GOING SOMEWHERE?!
NYAH

Part Seven

THE WAY OF TEA

SHHHHHHHHH
SHOPPING · PLAZA
ックス
松永商店
GALUMP GALUMP
HUH ?!
GALUMP
GAL-UMP GALUMP
GALUMP
WHEEEEN
GALUMP GALUMP
GYAK!!!

IT'S A WILD HORSE!
HO
AND RIDING IT...
BAKERY

...A DEAD MAN!
GALUMP
GALUMP
GALUMP
NO, WAIT!

HE'S JUST UNCONSCIOUS!
PROBABLY GOT DRUNK! THE JERK!

GALUMP
GALUMP
SPSH
SPSH
SPSH

GET AWAY!!
STOP FOLLOWING ME, SHAMPOO!
SPSH
SPSH
SPSH
MIEW
MIEW
MIEW

LOOK OUT!
THE HORSE IS ABOUT TO--
APPLE

WOOM
FOMP
KLONG
MIEW?
KREEE WHAK
SHHHHHH
SPSH SPSH
SPSH

HM ?
BINK
PLOP
HEY! YOU OKAY ?
WAPWAPWAP
......
GLINT
UHH...
BINK

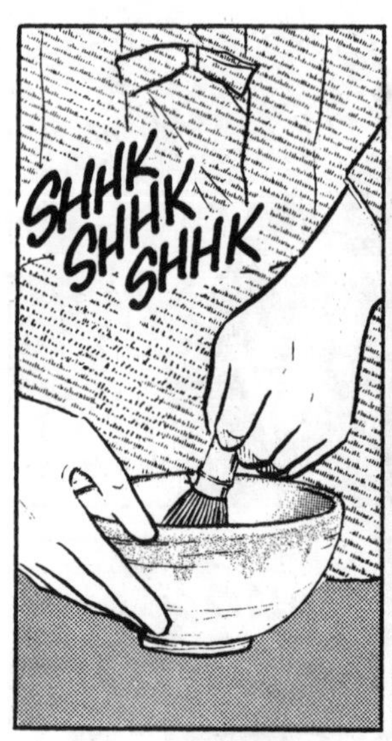
SHHK SHHK SHHK

PROFOUNDEST THANKS FOR SAVING THIS WORTHLESS LIFE.
THIS TEA MUST BE MY UNWORTHY GESTURE OF GRATITUDE.
HUH ?!

I REALLY DIDN'T DO ANYTHING TO BE THANKING ME FOR.
SKRITCH SKRITCH

TRUE. ONLY PREVENTED THIS LOWLY ONE'S DEATH.
BUT FOR THIS I BEG YOU PATHETICALLY TO TASTE OF MY GRATITUDE.
O-OKAY, WHATEVER.
GLMP

URK!
heh
heh heh heh
A PARALYSIS DRUG.
WHAT?!
SIGHH
OH, AT LAST, AT LAST, I HAVE MET A WOMAN OF STRENGTH!
SOB SOB SOB
WHALLA HELLA YOU TALL ALOUT?

HM ?
GALUMP GALUMP GALUMP
YOWL YOWL YOWL
GALUMP GALUMP
RANMA ?!
GALUMP GALUMP

HEY! WHERE ARE YOU GOING WITH RANMA?!
VISHHH

TONG

ping

PART TIME JOB!
PROPERTY
FOR SALE
GALUMP
GALUMP
GALUMP

WHO WAS THAT ?!
THIS IS A TEA-CEREMONY SPOON !
YOWL YOWL YOWL
GOZZZG

SHF SHF
SHF
AH
AH
CHOO!
A WEDDING KIMONO ?!
WHAT THE-- ?!

POW
AH. YOU HAVE AWAKENED.
I BEG FORGIVENESS FOR MY EXECRABLE RUDENESS.
WHO DO YOU THINK YOU ARE?!
NO, I BEG YOU! HEAR ME OUT!
PLEASE! I GROVEL! HEAR ME!
STOMP STOMP
I'M GONE!
SHHHHH

SENTARO!

SHK

SHK

WHOOSH

SHK

SHK

HAVE YOU FORCED ANOTHER POOR GIRL INTO THAT KIMONO AGAIN?!

ULP! GR-GRANDMOTHER?

SHE'S NOT JUST ANOTHER GIRL!

THIS IS THE GIRL I WILL MARRY!

UH... EXACTLY WHAT DO YOU THINK...

...YOU'RE TALKING ABOUT?!

BOOOM

NOW, IT WASN'T NICE TO DO THAT...

WHOOSH

...TO OUR ONLY HEIR!!
!
SHWAKK
TUMP
UGH!
KAPONK

WHAT...
...KINDA MOVE WAS THAT?!

DAIMONJI SCHOOL OF MARTIAL ARTS TEA CEREMONY.
THE NAPKIN STRIKE.

MARTIAL ARTS TEA CEREMONY... ?

Gonnnng
YES.

I AM THE SOLE SON AND HEIR TO THE DAIMONJI SCHOOL OF MARTIAL ARTS TEA CEREMONY.
NOW AN ARRANGEMENT HAS BEEN MADE TO WED THIS WORTHLESS SOUL TO ANOTHER, THAT A FUTURE HEIR MIGHT BE BORN.

ALAS, ALAS...
...THE WOMAN CHOSEN...

...I CANNOT BRING MY LOWLY HEART TO LIKE!
CUT THE TEARS!

IN ORDER TO NULLIFY THIS ARRANGEMENT, I MUST FIND A WOMAN WHO CAN DEFEAT MY BETROTHED IN A MARTIAL ARTS TEA CEREMONY.

COUNT ME OUT OF IT!

ZHOOP

HO HO HO HO HO HO!

DO YOU THINK A WEAKLING LIKE THIS COULD POSSIBLY WIN A CONTEST SO DEMANDING?

RK!

OKAY, OLD BAT...

...YOU LISTEN UP NOW!

Part Eight

MEET MISS SATSUKI

PLEASE HAVE A SEAT, RANMA.
GONNNNG

GREAT.
THE WATER'S JUST HOT ENOUGH.
I WILL EDUCATE YOU IN THE MARTIAL ARTS TEA CEREMONY.
AFTER YOU WIN THIS MATCH, YOU WILL BE MY NOBLE BRIDE.
YOU WILL BE FAR MORE BEAUTIFUL THAN MY LOWLY SELF DESERVES.
SPLISH
AND WHAT IF I DON'T FIT THE *GOWN* ANYMORE ?
VOOP
GYEEEEEEE!

GYEEEEEEE?

GYEEEEE...
PAT PAT

GYEE... EE... EE... EE!
OH, KNOCK IT OFF!!

I THOUGHT I'D FINALLY FOUND THE WOMAN TO RESCUE ME FROM MY DESERVED BUT HORRID FATE.
BOO HOO HOO
JUST GIVE UP AND MARRY THE GIRL.
SHKK
SHKK SHKK
ONLY A MAN WHO DOES NOT KNOW SATSUKI COULD LACERATE ME WITH SUCH CRUEL WORDS!
SATSUKI?

HUH?
RRG!
LET ME THROUGH!
STOP! WHO ARE YOU?!
STOMP STOMP

RANMA!!
I KNOW YOU'RE HERE SOMEWHERE!
STOMP STOMP

ARELESSLY...
DROPPED?

AND YOU CAME ALL THIS WAY TO RETURN IT TO ME?

YOU HAVE MY GRATITUDE!

WHOK

YOU WANT ME TO TAKE RANMA'S PLACE IN THE MARTIAL ARTS TEA CEREMONY?

WELL...I DO HAVE SOME EXPERIENCE WITH THE TEA CEREMONY.
DO TELL.

YES, PLEASE TELL ME ALL ABOUT IT!
YOU DON'T MEAN YOU BELIEVE HER?
SHUT UP, RANMA!
IT SO HAPPENS KASUMI TAUGHT ME WHEN I WAS LITTLE!
SO LET'S SEE YOU DO IT.

OH, THE GODS HAVE NOT FORSAKEN ME YET!
sigh...
sniff
AKANE WILL MAKE THE PERFECT WIFE FOR THIS UNWORTHY FOOL!

KLAK
POOF

SPLAP

WHIP
WHIP
SPLAP
SPLAP

YAAAAAA!
SHE'S GOOD, HUH?
BOO HOO HOO
BUT SHE'S JUST SO... CUTE!

JUST SIT BACK AND WATCH, AKANE.
I'LL TAKE CARE OF THE MATCH.
WHAT...?
WHO ELSE CAN HANDLE IT?
......
UNLESS, OF COURSE, YOU THINK YOU CAN TRAIN THE BIGGEST KLUTZ IN ALL OF JAPAN IN TIME FOR THE MATCH!
SO I'M A KLUTZ, AM I ?!
KONG
KONG
YOU... YOU ARE CORRECT, RANMA...
ONLY YOU HAVE A CHANCE TO WIN THIS MATCH FOR ME.
BUT I REFUSE TO MARRY YOU!
WHO SAID I WANT TO MARRY YOU ?!

THE MARTIAL ARTS TEA CEREMONY IS FOUNDED UPON SITTING.

"SITTING"?
ALL FIGHTING IS DONE FROM THE PROPER SITTING POSITION.
WHY IS THIS HOUSE SO LONG?

IF YOU ARE READY... FOLLOW ME.

WHISSSHHHHH

IT IS UNWISE TO RUN WITH YOUR HANDS.
WHISSHHH
PATTA PATTA
HOW CAN HE BE SO FAST... WHEN HE'S SITTING DOWN?!

YES, QUITE TRUE, BUT...
PATTA PATTA
SHUT UP! I'M KEEPING UP WITH YOU, AREN'T I?

...IF YOU CANNOT USE YOUR HANDS WHEN YOU NEED THEM...

...IT COULD BE PAINFUL!
BONG

WHAT WAZZAT FOR ?!
VOOM
UP

SHA

REMAIN PROPERLY SEATED!
KLONG
WOK

HUH ?!
EH? GRANDMOTHER?
HO HO HO HO HO! THE CLUMSY GIRL CAN'T EVEN SIT CORRECTLY! HO HO!

DO YOU TRULY BELIEVE YOU CAN DEFEAT MISS SATSUKI IN TOMORROW'S MATCH?
TOMORROW ?!
WHAT ?!
IS *THAT* THE PROPER SITTING POSITION ?!

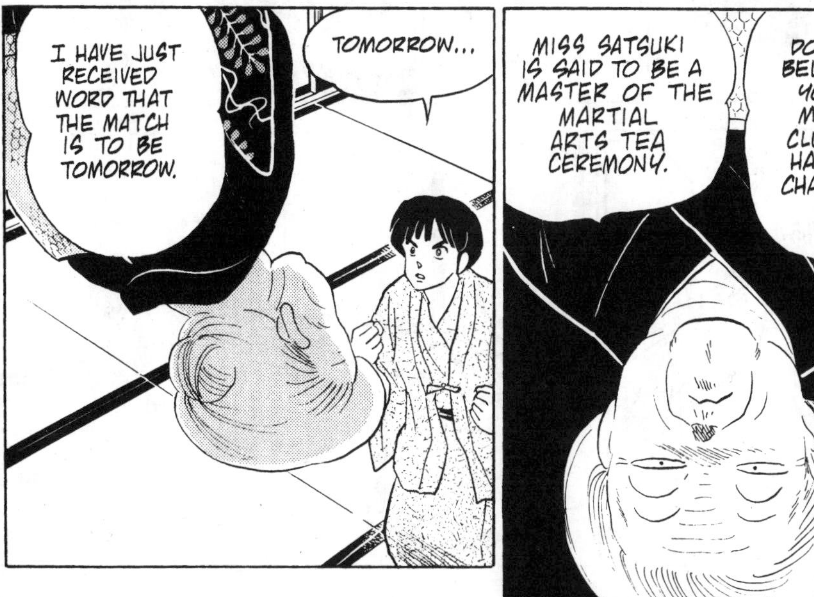

HOHOHOHOHOHO
I, FOR ONE, WILL BE LOOKING FORWARD TO THIS MATCH!
TOMORROW...
.....

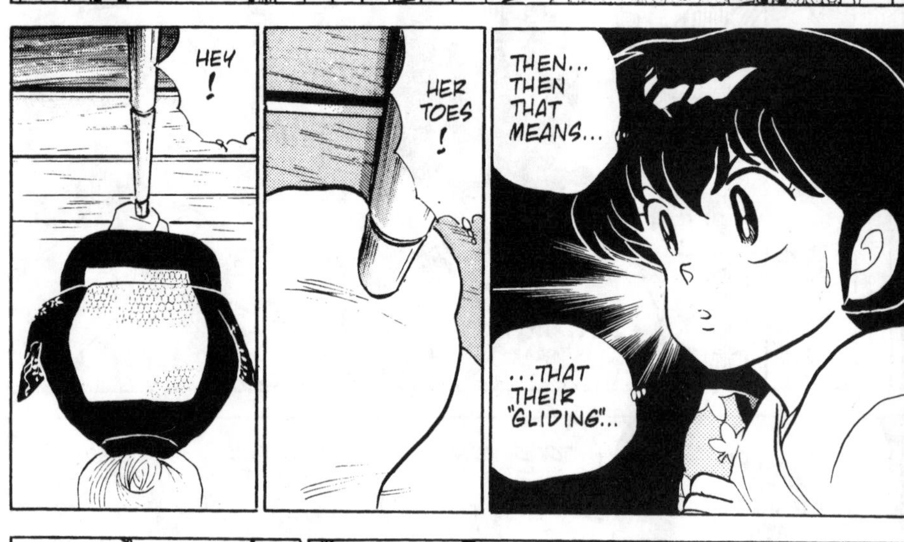
HEY!
HER TOES!
THEN... THEN THAT MEANS...
...THAT THEIR "GLIDING"...

...IS REALLY JUST RUNNING...
PUTT
PUTT PUTT
...LIKE THIS!
TOMORROW...

YOU MUST TRAIN! TRAIN UNTIL YOU DROP!!

SPLAT
ENOUGH IS ENOUGH!!

EVER SINCE YOU FOUND OUT I WAS A GUY YOU'VE BEEN LAYING INTO ME!
KICKING IS NOT PERMITTED!

I'M SICK OF IT!
WHOK
BOP
YAWN

GONNNNG
CHIRP CHIRP

HEH. SH-SHOWED... YOU... DIDN'T I?
PANT PANT PANT
HUFF HUFF HUFF HUFF
Y-YOU HAVE... MUH-MASTERED THE...TECHNIQUES... OF THE...MUH... MUH...YOU KNOW.

BY THE WAY...
WHAT KIND OF GIRL IS THIS "MISS SATSUKI" YOU'RE ENGAGED TO, ANYWAY?
SHE IS THE DAUGHTER OF THE MIYAKOJI SCHOOL OF MARTIAL ARTS TEA CEREMONIES. SHE WAS ALSO... AHEM...

...MISS TEA CEREMONY FOR 1993.
"MISS..."? SHE MUST BE A BABE!

SHE MUST HAVE A HORRIBLE PERSONALITY.
WELL, IN TRUTH...
SHE'S VERY BRIGHT AND SOCIABLE.
WHAT?!

SO HOW COME YOU DON'T LIKE HER ?!
TOURNAMENT SITE

MEET MISS SATSUKI.
IK IK IK.
KLONK

PART NINE
PROPOSAL ACCEPTED

YOU'VE GOT TO BE KIDDING.

I'M *OUTTA* HERE!

BUT YOU CAN'T!

YOU'VE COME THIS FAR...!

Z-Z-Z.

LIKE HELL I CAN'T!

STOMP STOMP

ME! RANMA! FIGHTING A *MONKEY*!

YAWN

ITCH ITCH

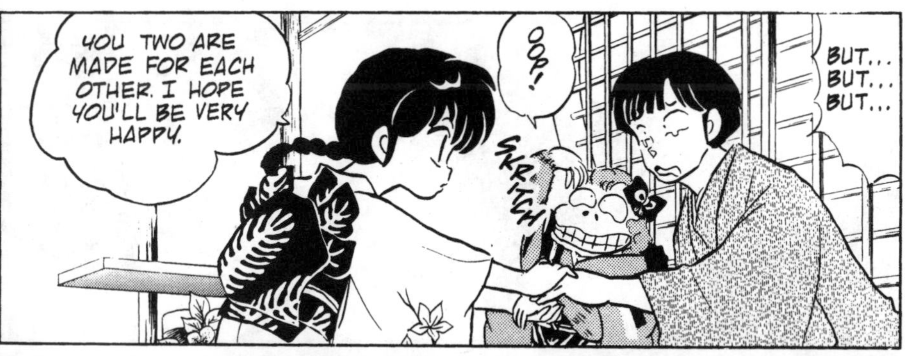
BUT...
BUT...
BUT...
OOF!
SKRITCH
YOU TWO ARE MADE FOR EACH OTHER. I HOPE YOU'LL BE VERY HAPPY.

INVITE ME TO THE WEDDING!

EEEEEEEE
WAK WAK WAK
WAK WAK

BONG

SNK SNK.
WHAT THE-- ?!

HEH.

YOU'RE DEAD, FURBALL!

VOOM

EEEE

OH, RANMA! THEN YOU **WILL** FIGHT FOR ME!

sigh...

TEA-SPOON DARTS!

VSSHHH VSSHHH VSSHHH

TOK TOK TOK TOK TOK

IP!

THAP

PUF
AUGH!
THE TEA-POWDER MIST TECHNIQUE!
BLONNG
FOLLOWED BY THE POT-STRIKE! OH, WHAT A DOUBLE-WHAMMY!
FONK
POT COUNTER-STRIKE!
LADLE-STRIKE!
TONG TONG
EEK EEK

THIS MISS CLUMSY ISN'T SO BAD AFTER ALL.
GYAAAH!!
EEEK
EEEK
EEEK
SHE HOLDS HER OWN AGAINST MISS SATSUKI'S BEST MOVES.

WITH THIS MUCH SKILL...
GRR! GRR!
...SHE PROVES HERSELF A WORTHY BRIDE FOR YOU, SENTARO.
OOP! OOP!

WELL, SENTARO?
WHAT DO YOU THINK?

SENTARO?

BUT WHY IN THE WORLD...
EEK
EEK
GRR
GRR
GRR

I HAVE NO IDEA.
...ARE YOU ENGAGED TO A MONKEY?!

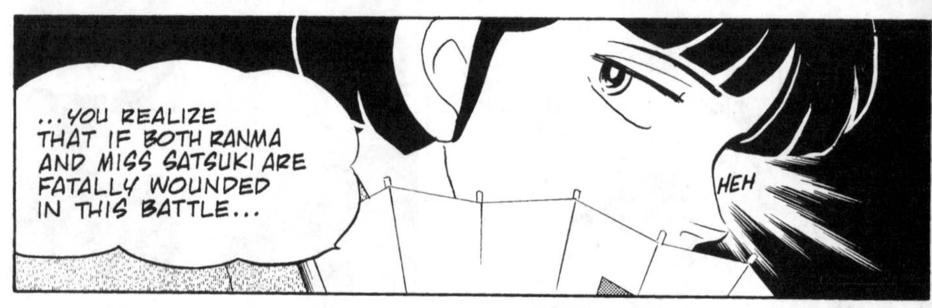

...NO ONE WOULD STAND IN THE WAY OF OUR MARRIAGE!

YOU CAN'T BE SERIOUS.

CONGRATULAT-IONS

WHAMMO
THOMP
SO, IT ALL COMES CLEAR NOW!
WHOK
WH-WHATEVER DO YOU MEAN?

GET BACK HERE, FLEA-PICKER!
WHOOP
SWISH
HYAH!
VISH
TOK TOK TOK TOK
KRAK

DOUBLE-DECKER POT-STRIKE!
VOOP
KEE KEE!
WHACH
TNG
TNG
SHK SHK SHK
YOU TRYIN' TO MESS ME UP?
RRIP
CARE FOR SOME TEA?

NOW I MAY FINISH YOU BOTH OFF...

...AND MAKE A WIFE...

...OF THE NOBLE AKANE!

SHHM

BOOT

IN YOUR DREAMS !!

THOP

WHUMP

ARE YOU... ALL RIGHT?
OHHH...

WHAT...?

HWOOOP!

OH, POOR SANAE! I'M SO SORRY!
S...SANAE...?
OOP OOP

I'M SORRY I ASKED YOU TO TAKE MY PLACE, SANAE!
IT MUST HAVE BEEN TERRIBLE FOR YOU!
SNIF SNIF
EEP

THEN... THEN YOU MUST BE...
TAKE HER PLACE?

GYEEEEEE!!
I AM.
...THE REAL MISS SATSUKI!

I...
I...
WHEN THE DAY FINALLY CAME...

W-WELL...I WAS SO LOOKING FORWARD TO MEETING MY FUTURE HUSBAND... BUT...
AND JUST HOW DID THIS ODD CIRCUMSTANCE COME TO BE, DEAR?

YOU THOUGHT IT WAS LESS EMBARRASSING TO SEND A MONKEY IN YOUR PLACE ?!
HOW DEMURE AND MAIDENLY OF YOU!
...I WAS JUST SO EMBARRASSED!
SIGH
BOO HOO

DEAR RANMA,
I THANK YOU FOR THE UNDESERVED JOY THAT THIS LOWLY ONE NOW RELISHES.
Leaving on our honeymoon
WE WILL PROBABLY NEVER MEET AGAIN...

MY, MY! IS THAT A RUNAWAY HORSE ?
GET OFFA MY HEAD!
SNORT
STOMP
OR SO I THOUGHT.
BUT ISN'T FATE MIRACULOUS ?

Part Ten

It's Fast or It's Free

PLEASE, UPPERCLASSMAN KUNO!
OH, UPPERCLASSMAN KUNO!
A Gift for You
福
AND AKANE TENDO!
MM...?
THE PIGTAILED GIRL!
HMMMMMM...
WHICH OF US DO YOU LOVE?
YOU HAVE TO DECIDE, UPPERCLASSMAN!

I LOVE YOU BO--
BE-BAP

YOU HAVE TO CHOOSE...
...JUST ONE OF US!

WHAP

CREEK
HM?

MMMMMMMMMM
CHIRP CHIRP

VOOM
VVVVVOOOOM
TENDO TRAINING HALL
VOOOOOM
VVV-
VVV-
VVV-
GREETINGS!
VREEECH
SPTTT!!

AKANE TENDO...
I HAVE COME TO GIVE YOU YOUR ANSWER!
MY... WHAT?
WHAT ARE YOU TALKING ABOUT?

YO, KUNO!
WHAT'S UP, MAN?
VWIP
WHONK

HEY!
DID I TELL YOU TRAINING SESSION WAS OVER?!
WOOM
SPLAT

WATCH IT, OLD MAN! THAT HURT!
BAPPITA BAPPITA BAPPITA
AS I WAS SAYING...

I HAVE DECIDED!
IT IS TIME I CHOSE MY TRUE AND ONLY LOVE!

TAKE THESE ROSES AS PROOF OF MY ARDOR.
HERE, DAD. YOU'RE IT.
VIP
VIP

IT IS NOT YOU TO WHOM I PLEDGE MY LOVE!
MY HEART DOESN'T EXACTLY FLUTTER FOR YOU, EITHER!
SSSSSS

INSTEAD OF PINING FOR A MYSTERY-GIRL WHO, LIKE THE WIND...
...APPEARS AND VANISHES AND CANNOT BE CAUGHT...

...I CHOOSE YOU, AKANE, WHO IS ALWAYS CLOSE AT HAND.
HOW FLATTERING.
SPLASH
CHOMP
CHOMP
CHOMP

BLOOSH

P-TUI!

TH-THE PIGTAILED GIRL...!

WELL, THERE'S YOUR WIND, KUNO!

DRIP DROP DRIP

RRRIP
AARGH!!

SHFF

SHFF

YOU SHALL BOTH COME TO MY RESIDENCE NEXT SUNDAY!
SQUIRT

YES! I HAVE IT!

I CANNOT BEAR TO LOSE EITHER!
WHAT'S WITH HIM?
BEATS ME.

WHICHEVER ARRIVES FIRST SHALL HAVE ME!
IT MUST BE THUS!
PLEASE FORGIVE ME!
BUT I HAVE NO OTHER CHOICE!
WHAT... IN THE *WORLD*...
...ARE YOU *TALKING ABOUT?!*
POW
HA HA HA
I SHALL BE WAITING!

IT BATTLE BETWEEN WOMANS?
RIGHT.
THE FIRST DELIVERY GIRL TO REACH THE TARGET HOUSE WINS.
THE RACE'LL BE NEXT SUNDAY.
WELL, YOU KNOW...
BARBEQUE EELS
SCRAPE
...I DO HATE TO BRAG, BUT...
...MY SHAMPOO HERE...
VVP
VVP
...IS NOT A BAD MARTIAL ARTIST HERSELF.
FWISH
NOODLE COMBINATION.

FRY RICE WITH WONTON.
....
EELS

TAK
TAK
TAK

EASY-WIN RACE IS NO FUN FOR SHAMPOO!
ARE YOU SURE YOU WANT HER TO COMPETE?

OUR DELIVERY GIRLS ARE NO SLOUCHES!
DON'T WORRY ABOUT US.
SLURRRP

ME? ENTER THIS "MISS MARTIAL ARTS TAKEOUT" CONTEST?

WHY IN THE WORLD DO I HAVE TO...

AH. NOW I GET IT.

WHAGGA YOU MEAM?

SELLING OUT YOUR OWN DAUGHTER FOR AN ORDER OF EEL TERIYAKI. SHAME ON YOU.

I DID NO SUCH THING!

PLASH

If he wins it's free ramen for a year, right?

THAT'S ONE HEALTHY-LOOKIN' GIRL YOU'VE GOT, MISTER!

SLURP

HALF THAT RAMEN'S **MINE**, OLD MAN!

FUTONS

Fweee

Pop

Pop

OH, RANMA!

SHAMPOO KNEW YOU WILL COME!

DIDN'T HAVE ANYTHING BETTER TO DO...

Miss

House of Ramen

AL ARTS

KEOUT

VROOM

VROOM

VROOM

CAT CAFE

PIZZA

MINI MART
ABC CAFE
PLAZA
WOW, AKANE, YOU LOOK GREAT!
THINK SO?

AND AT THAT LUCKY ADDRESS...

PIGTAILED GIRL...

AKANE TENDO...

PLEASE DO NOT HATE ME IF YOU ARE NOT CHOSEN!

Part Eleven

EYES ON THE PRIZE

THE ANYTHING-GOES MISS MARTIAL ARTS TAKEOUT RACE IS ABOUT TO BEGIN!
ON YOUR MARKS...
GOOOO
VROOOM
HYAAAH
HYAAAH

House of Ramen
Koga BOOK
BOOKS
THEY CAN MOVE !
WHOA !
OFFICE SUPPLIES

ONLY ONES WITH CHANCE TO WIN IS US BOTH!

AREN'T YOU FORGETTING SOMEONE ?

SHOOM

I'M GOING TO WIN THIS RACE!

SHMMMM

IN MARTIAL ARTS TAKEOUT...

...THERE NO RULES!

TINK

ATTACK IS ALL OKAY!

JAB

YOW!

IQUOR

ELECTRONICS

BE

WOOOM

THOK

Salon Eve

HAPPY

PRODUCE

OODLES O' NOODLES

NOT BAD!

WHAT TECHNIQ !

MY OWN PATENTED "BOX-BLOWER BLOW"!

POIK

BOING

YEEEE!

WHEN IT COMES TO MARTIAL ARTS TAKEOUT...

...NOT EVEN YOU CAN BEAT MY SHAMPOO!

HA HA HA HA HA

HEH! TALK IS CHEAP!

I WOULDN'T WANT TO WIN THIS TOO EASY, ANYWAY!

THEN IF SHAMPOO WIN, YOU DATE WITH SHAMPOO ?
SURE THING. ANYTHING YOU WANT...IF YOU BEAT ME!
RANMA!

CAT AFE
VISH
WOOP!
House of Ramen
WOOP!
House of Ramen
BOOM
EEP!
PIZZA

YAA!
BOOM
WAA!
BOOM
BOOM
HEE HEE
Curry Kitchen
SUSHI HUT
TEMPURA TIME
Mr. Sukiyaki

HONESTLY, RANMA. YOU'RE SUCH A SUCKER FOR THESE THINGS.
BWAH HA HA!
BOOM BOOM
EEK EEK

THE KUNO HOUSE...
AKANE TENDO... PIGTAILED GIRL...
WHICH OF YOU WILL JUMP INTO THESE ARMS FIRST?
TRULY, I CANNOT LIVE WITHOUT EITHER!
AND YET... AND YET...
I MUST CHOOSE THE WINNER!
FORGIVE ME, LADIES!
SOB
SOB

House of Ramen

VISH

WHOOP!

RANMA! YOU NO WANT TO DATE SHAMPOO SO MUCH?!
huf huf
CAT CAFE
TOP
DON'T BE STUPID!
House of Ramen
TUP
ALL YOU HAVE TO DO IS SPILL MY BOWL!
VISH
VISH
WOOP.
Ramen
WOOP.
WOOP.
CAT CAFE
House of Ramen

THOP!
NO!
JUST KIDDING!
VIP

BOO HOO HOO!
HEY! WAIT!
YOU DON'T HAVE TO CRY!
HEH!

TAK
YOW!
POK POK
KRAKKLE..
BLOOM
C-C-C-COLD!!

MEOW
EEEE-YAAAA!
YAAAA!!
MYEW
YAAA!
YAAAA!
MYEW
SHOOOM
GOMP
......
FWAP FWAP FWAP FWAP FW

R!P

FLING
MYEW?

WAP WAP
WAP

ARE YOU OKAY ?
UH?

MY RAMEN !
BOING

YAAAA!
OOOOO

NO! NO! NO!
UMM
OH !

HEY, NO FAIR! I DIDN'T SAVE YOU SO YOU'D BEAT ME!

SHMMM

TOOM

TOOM

KLOP

THAT'S THE HOUSE!

I WON'T LOSE!

SHOOOM

OOOOOO

SLAM
FOOD DELIVERY!

RIP
BOOM
NIHAO!
KUH...
KUNO?!
WHOP
TAKEOUT'S HERE.

To be continued!
NOW THE *MARTIAL* PART WILL REALLY BEGIN.
AMAZING! A THREE-WAY TIE!

Part Twelve

NOODLES, ANYONE?

NOW THE MISS MARTIAL ARTS TAKEOUT CONTEST COMES TO ITS CLIMAX!

WHAT IS THAT IDIOT *KUNO* DOING HERE?!

DON'T ASK ME.

WHUMP
I NEVER DREAMED YOU BOTH LOVED ME SO MUCH!
BRRRR
BOOM
AND JUST *WHAT*--
--DO YOU THINK YOU'RE *DOIN'*?!
BOING
EH?
SWISH
I WIN RACE!
Y-YOU ARE IN LOVE WITH ME, TOO?!

VOOM
OH NO, YOU DON'T!!
GLOMP
KUNO'S GONNA EAT *MY* RAMEN!
VOOP
KOP
I'VE DECIDED.
YOU SHALL HAVE ME!
SO WHO ***WANTS*** YOU?!
HWEEEEE
THAT'S IT...RIGHT THIS WAY...

JAB
FOR YOU--I SHALL!
HAVE SOME EEL, KUNO!
!
!
RAR
VISH
YOU NO DO THAT!
I WIN RACE, I AM DATE WITH RANMA!
NO ONE STOP SHAMPOO NOW!
VOOM
TAP
WHSH
Top
WHP

MARTIAL ARTS TAKEOUT SPECIAL ATTACK!
FOOOP
HERE IT COMES!
CHOW MEIN STRIKE!
GHHHHHHHH
EM?!
THE CHOW MEIN! IT'S MOVING LIKE A SNAKE!
THOSE EXTRA-CHEWY NOODLES ARE A SPECIALTY OF THE CAT CAFE!
GASP!
IT'S NEARLY IMPOSSIBLE TO ESCAPE THEIR GRASP.
ONCE MY CHOW MEIN HAS YOU--IT'S ALL OVER!

P-PIGTAILED GIRL...

YOU TOOK MY PLACE... TO SAVE ME?

I WILL *SAVE* YOU, MY LOVE!

I WILL *EAT* THIS CHOW MEIN!

SOB

VOOM

BONNNG
HURRY, RANMA! EAT THAT STUFF!
KREEK
SHLOOP
KLAK
LIKE USUAL, RANMA...
VRRRR
...YOU *TOO* GOOD!
RRRRRROOO
HUH?!

OOOP!

OH!!

WHAT THE--?!

YAAAA!

SINCE YOU ALL WANT ME SO DESPERATELY...
TO TAKE FOOD FROM ANY ONE OF YOU WOULD INSULT THE OTHERS.
THIS LEAVES ONLY ONE CHOICE.
WE MUST ALL LIVE HERE TOGETH--
BOP

OPENING!

VISH

POK

NO!

WHOA!

CATCH IT, RANMA! PLEASE!!

VRRRRR

WELL...I GUESS SO...

TIK

VOOM

MGH?
plop

MP MP
MP
MP

GULP

NO MORE EEL.
AKANE DISQUALIFIED!
HEH

WHY...
...YOU...
GRRRR

AKANE GO HOME WITH TAIL BETWEEN LEGS!
NYAHH!
TROMP TROMP

HM?

TANK!
WAX

AKANE... D-DON'T...
SHAMPOO...

WANNA BE A *CAT?!*

HOP!

SPLASH

STOP IT, AKANE!

GLOMP
YOW!
PLOOSH
HEY!

OH, RANMA SAVE SHAMPOO! SHAMPOO SO HAPPY!
TEE-HEE

Part Thirteen
I WON'T EAT IT!

BLOOGH
EE-E-YAAAA!!
PSHHHH
YOU WON'T GET AWAY!
RRREEM
RANMA KEEP RUNNING AND DATE WITH SHAMPOO!

POOM
PSHHH
WHAT ARE YOU *THINKING* OF?!
WHY ARE YOU SIDING WITH *SHAMPOO?!*
KROMP

BLOOMP OOMP OOMP

HUH?

RK RK RK

BLOO

SHH

AK!

YAAAAA!!

MYOW!

TWEET TWEET

YOWR
GRAB
AARRRGH!

FRAK
EXIT
MYEW MYEW
YOWWW!
DOWN TO DOJO
VROOOOM
MYEW MYEW
EE-GAAA!!

IT SOUNDS AS THOUGH THE MARTIAL ARTS TAKEOUT BATTLE HAS MOVED!
JUST A MOMENT...
VROOOOM
HEE-YAGGA!

VROOOOM
湯殿

SPLASH
BONK

BLORSH

BLOOSHHH

KRAK

BURBBLE

SPLISH SPLASH

WHA...?

PLOOSH!

SHAMPOO'S CHOW MEIN ALL *GONE!!*

GUH.

SHLP
FIRST OFF, PUT THIS ON!

OH, SO TERRIBLE! NOW SHAMPOO NO CAN DATE WITH RANMA!
GLOMP
WHOA WHOA WHOA WHOA!

JUST DO IT!
IF I DO, RANMA DATE WITH SHAMPOO?

WHISHH
YOIKS!

HOOOOO

RANMA SAOTOME...

YOU DARE TAKE SUCH LASCIVIOUS ACTION IN THE BATHTUB OF MY RESIDENCE?

OH, PLEASE.

R·B·QUE EEL

YOUR REWARD, VULGAR WRETCH!

OH, STUFF IT!

BLOOP

...WE COULD *END* THIS LUNACY!
FASH
WHAT ARE YOU TALKING ABOUT?
VIP
BE A GOOD BOY AND EAT!
YOU'VE GONE MAD!
BLISH
SPLISH
I, TATEWAKI KUNO, AM NOT ONE TO EAT FROM THE HAND OF JUST ANY MAN!
HE NO KNOW THAT BOY-TYPE AND GIRL-TYPE RANMA IS SAME PERSON?

MY ONLY DESIRE FOR YOUR SOGGY RAMEN...
...IS TO *DESTROY* IT!

STRIKE STRIKE
STRIKE STRIKE
STRIKE STRIKE
STRIKE STRIKE!

WHOA.

WHOA.

WHOA.

WHOA.

HYAHH!

WHISH

VOOM

SPECIAL DELIVERY STRIKE!

WHA--?

SNAG
PUPPET GRIP!
UNGH!

MMPH
YOU'RE MINE! EAT IT!

RANMA SUCH AMATEUR FOR MARTIAL ART TAKEOUT!

HEH...
LIKE WHAT ?
PUPPET GRIP HAVE ONE BIG FLAW!

YOU MAY HAVE TAKEN CONTROL OF MY ARMS...
CAN'T YOU SEE IT, FOOL?!

HA
HA
HA
WHA
...BUT UNLESS YOU CAN MAKE ME OPEN MY MOUTH, YOU CANNOT MAKE ME *EAT!*

OH, NO!
YOU'RE RIGHT!

HEH HEH
HEH HEH.
.....
SSWIRL
GRM
GRM
GRM
GRM
A GIANT...
WATER-
SPOUT?
YOW!
GOOSH
BLOO

OOSHHH
A LOT OF WATER!
WATER!
WHAT ARE YOU DOING?!
I WOULD RATHER DROWN THAN BE FED BAD RAMEN BY A MAN!
HWEEEEEE
PLASH
PFFFT!

END. RANMA 1/2 GRAPHIC NOVEL VOL. 5